WE WEAR PANTS

KATIE ABEY

BLOOMSBURY
CHILDREN'S BOOKS
LONDON OXFORD NEW YORK NEW DELHI SYDNEY

We Wear Pants

Who is sitting on the toilet?

Which animals are **wearing** pants? Find your **favourites**!

Ants in my pants!
Rocking around in my pants
Not me, I'm wearing wellies!
Pants dance
¿&? !0 Greetings!
Penguin pants
Superhero pants
How do you wear yours?
Hide-and-seek pants
Matching pants

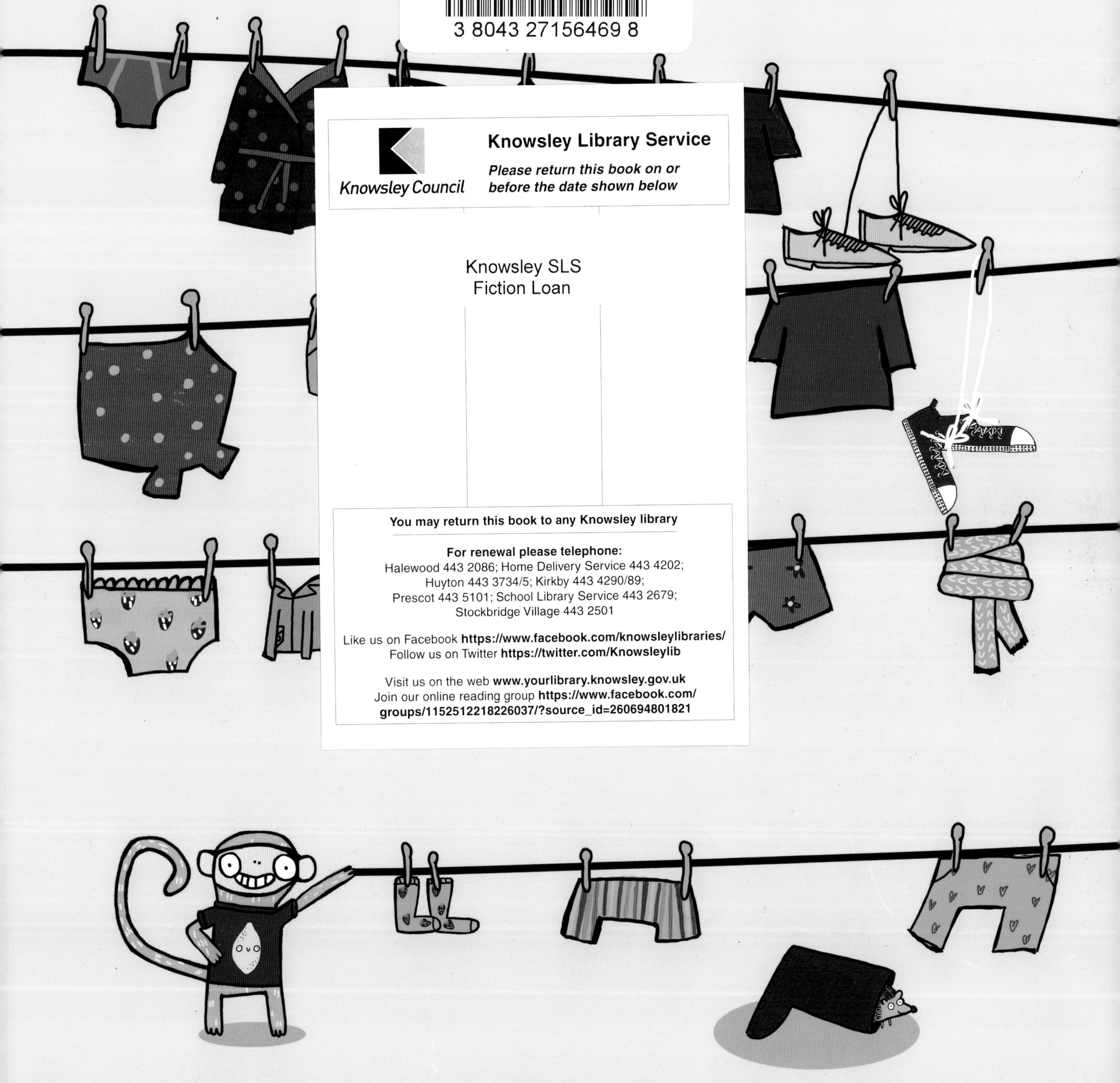

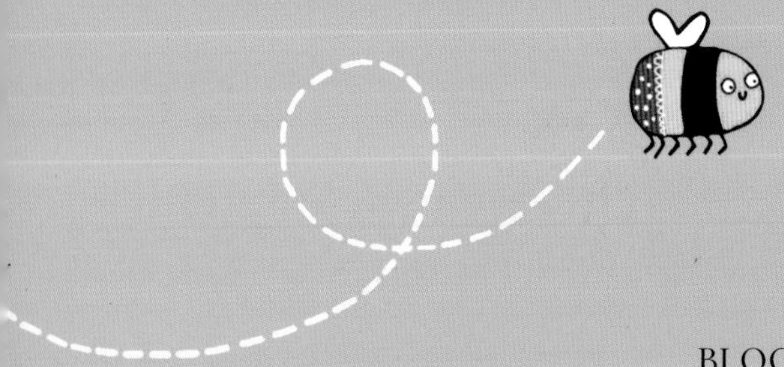

For Isla May

BLOOMSBURY CHILDREN'S BOOKS
Bloomsbury Publishing Plc
50 Bedford Square, London, WC1B 3DP, UK

BLOOMSBURY, BLOOMSBURY CHILDREN'S BOOKS and the Diana logo are trademarks of Bloomsbury Publishing Plc

First published in Great Britain 2018 by Bloomsbury Publishing Plc

A catalogue record for this book is available from the British Library

ISBN: HB: 978-1-4088-9818-5 PB: 978-1-4088-9360-9

2 4 6 8 10 9 7 5 3 1

Printed and bound in China by Leo Paper Products, Heshan, Guangdong

To find out more about our authors and books visit www.bloomsbury.com and sign up for our newsletters
To find out more about Katie Abey visit www.katieabey.co.uk

So don't forget your pants!
Pull your pants up
Paaaaaaaaaants
Windy pants
Looking snappy in my nappy
Pants keep your bottom covered
Funny pants
Wait... these are too big
I water plants in my pants
Pant-tastic!

We Wear Wellies

Who has the funniest wellies?

Waterproof wombat
Count the rubber ducks
Impostor!
Muddy paws
Who has tall wellies?
Not me, I'm wearing a hat!
Oh no!
Splish splash
Oops!
Wellies are fun
Wellies keep our feet dry

Tall wellies
Ahoy!
Where are my wellies?
Got one!
BEARy muddy
I'll help you
So don't forget your wellies!

We Wear Hats

Choose a hat and find your **favourite** animal.

Can you put your hat on all by yourself?

We wear hats in the winter
My hat keeps my ear warm
Holiday hat
My hat is for bedtime
Find a tiny fish and I will eat my hat
Anyone for tea?
Find my twin
Count the hats

Whose hat can you eat?
Not me, I'm wearing a coat!
Time for an adventure!
Who is the biggest animal?
My hat keeps the rain off
Do you like my hat?
Swimming hat
Party time!
So don't forget your hat!

We Wear Coats

What are all the animals **doing?**

Count the umbrellas
Bus Stop
Home time!
Nice weather for ducks
Hood-hog
Who has the same coat as me?
We are dressed as each other

Who is driving the bus?
A goat in a coat?
We wear coats to keep us dry
Not me, I'm wearing shorts!
Water fight
So don't forget your coat!
Quick run!
Spotty coat

We Wear Shorts

Who is wearing shorts on a sunny day?

Shorts cover up your pants
Have a picnic in your shorts
Not me, I'm wearing glasses!
Please help me put my sun cream on.
Who is wearing banana shorts?
Even dragons wear shorts

Picnic time
Shorts snap!
So don't forget your shorts!
Surf's up
Shorts dance
Time to put my shorts on
Horsing around
I'll eat my shorts

We Wear Glasses

Who has the **best** glasses?

Do you wear glasses?
Glasses help you see better
C
AN
YOU READ
THIS SMALL TEXT?
Eye test
Not me, I'm wearing a scarf!
I sssssseeeeee!
Off to work
Where are my glasses?
Look out!
I wear goggles
Cracking
Movie time
Do these look too big?

Weeeeeee
Magnified
Reading glasses
Four eyes are better than two
Oops!
I'm cool
Who has the smallest glasses?
So don't forget your glasses!
Choose a pair...
My glasses protect my eyes

We Wear Scarves

Which scarf would you wear?

My scarf is too small
Chilly!
Which one?
I live in my scarf
Scarf skipping
Toasty
Follow my scarf
Peekaboo!
My scarf is too big

How many stripy scarves are there?
Wrap up warm
Not me, I'm wearing socks!
Got you!
Hey!
Sloth angel
Monster scarf
Scarf skating
Who has the same scarf as me?
So don't forget your scarf!

We Wear Socks

What are these animals **wearing?**

Socks are for feet
Croc in a sock
Urgh smelly!
OOPS! Too big!
Twinkle socks
Not me, I'm wearing shoes!
Who is on my sock?

My socks are red and green
So am I!
Odd socks
Where has my other sock gone?
How many socks?
Long socks
So don't forget your socks!
Socks are warm
I am putting my socks on
I live in my sock
Sausage socks
Stripy socks

We Wear Shoes

Choose a pair of shoes. **Count** the green shoes.

Shoes protect our feet

Who has odd shoes?
Shoe shopping
My shoes make me tall
Frog in a clog
I prefer the shoebox
Horse shoes
Silly shoes!

How many shoes?
Not me, I’m wearing a t-shirt!
Flipper fun!
Who has sandals?
Car boot
I want those shoes
So don’t forget your shoes!
Cosy

We Wear T-shirts

What are all the animals **doing** at the fair?

Count all the candy floss
Not me, I'm wearing pyjamas!
Croc top-croc
I prefer a woolly jumper
Hi guys!
Spotty t-shirt

I love my t-shirt
Yarrr!
Weeee!
BEE brave
So don't forget your t-shirt!
My t-shirt is too long
Yum
Goat-TEE
Don't drop your ice cream!
Bear with me

We Wear Pyjamas

Goodnight animals. Don't **forget** your pyjamas!

Put your pyjamas on for story time!
Zzzzzz
FAIRY tired
Boo!
Sleepy snake
Who is dreaming?
Zzzzzz
Not me, I'm wearing pants!
Zzzzzz
Hot dog

Shhhh!
Wake up!
Exhausted emu
Zzzzzz
Zzzzzz
Who is sleeping upside down?
Zzzzzz
Time to brush my teeth
Zzzzzz

We All Get Dressed

What will YOU wear today?
Even me!